Lion

Bobcat

Panther

Tiger

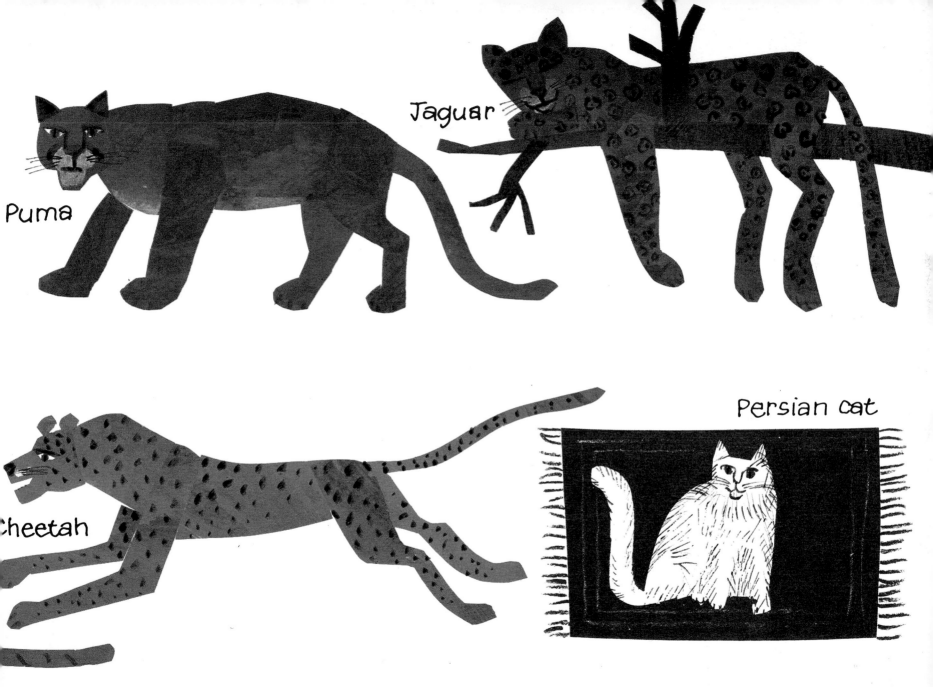

Puma

Jaguar

Cheetah

Persian cat

Dedicated to all the cats in my life

Eric Carle Have you seen my cat?

SCHOLASTIC INC.
New York Toronto London Auckland Sydney

Have you seen my cat?

Have you seen my cat?

Have you seen
my cat?

This is not <u>my</u> cat!

This is not my cat!

This is not <u>my</u> cat!

Have you seen my cat?

This is not <u>my</u> cat!

Have you seen my cat?

This is not <u>my</u> cat!

Where is my cat?

Have you seen my cat?

ISBN 0-590-44461-1

12 11 10 9 8 7 6 5 4 3   1 2 3 4 5 6/9
                    Printed in the U.S.A.   08
            First Scholastic printing, March 1991

Lion.

Bobcat.

Panther

Tiger

Puma

Jaguar

Cheetah

Persian cat